Balloon Toons®

PRICKLES
vs. The Dust Bunnies

Daniel Cleary

🍎 BLUE APPLE BOOKS

Copyright © 2011 Daniel Cleary
Balloon Toons® is a registered
trademark of Harriet Ziefert, Inc.
All rights reserved/CIP data is available.
Published in the United States 2011 by
🍎 Blue Apple Books
515 Valley Street, Maplewood, NJ 07040
www.blueapplebooks.com

First Edition
Printed in China
HC ISBN: 978-1-60905-080-1
2 4 6 8 10 9 7 5 3 1
PB ISBN: 978-1-60905-185-3
2 4 6 8 10 9 7 5 3 1

What's to be afraid of?

It's a beautiful day.

There's nothing out there but a yard full of green grass.

Grass scares us.

So what if we're a little fuzzy looking and have a few funny spots and speckles. Nobody's perfect.

We're real.

We're interesting.

We're organic.

We're made from all kinds of neat stuff.

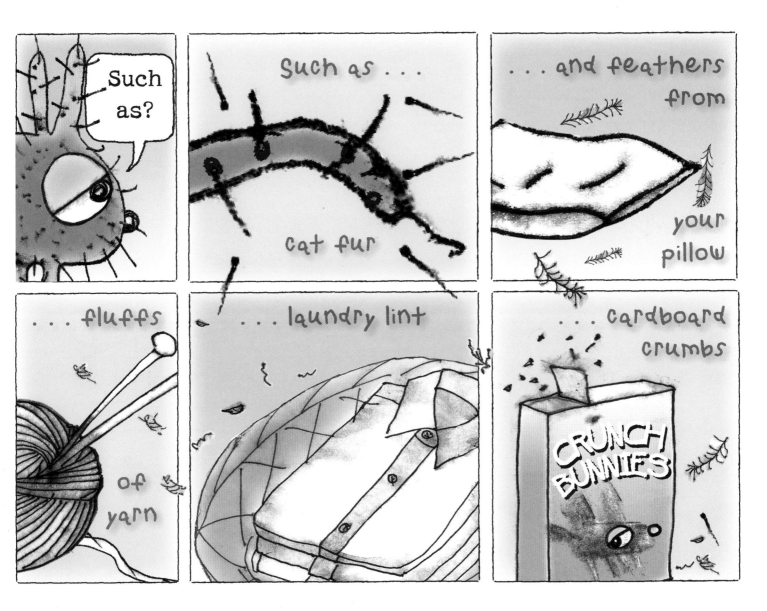

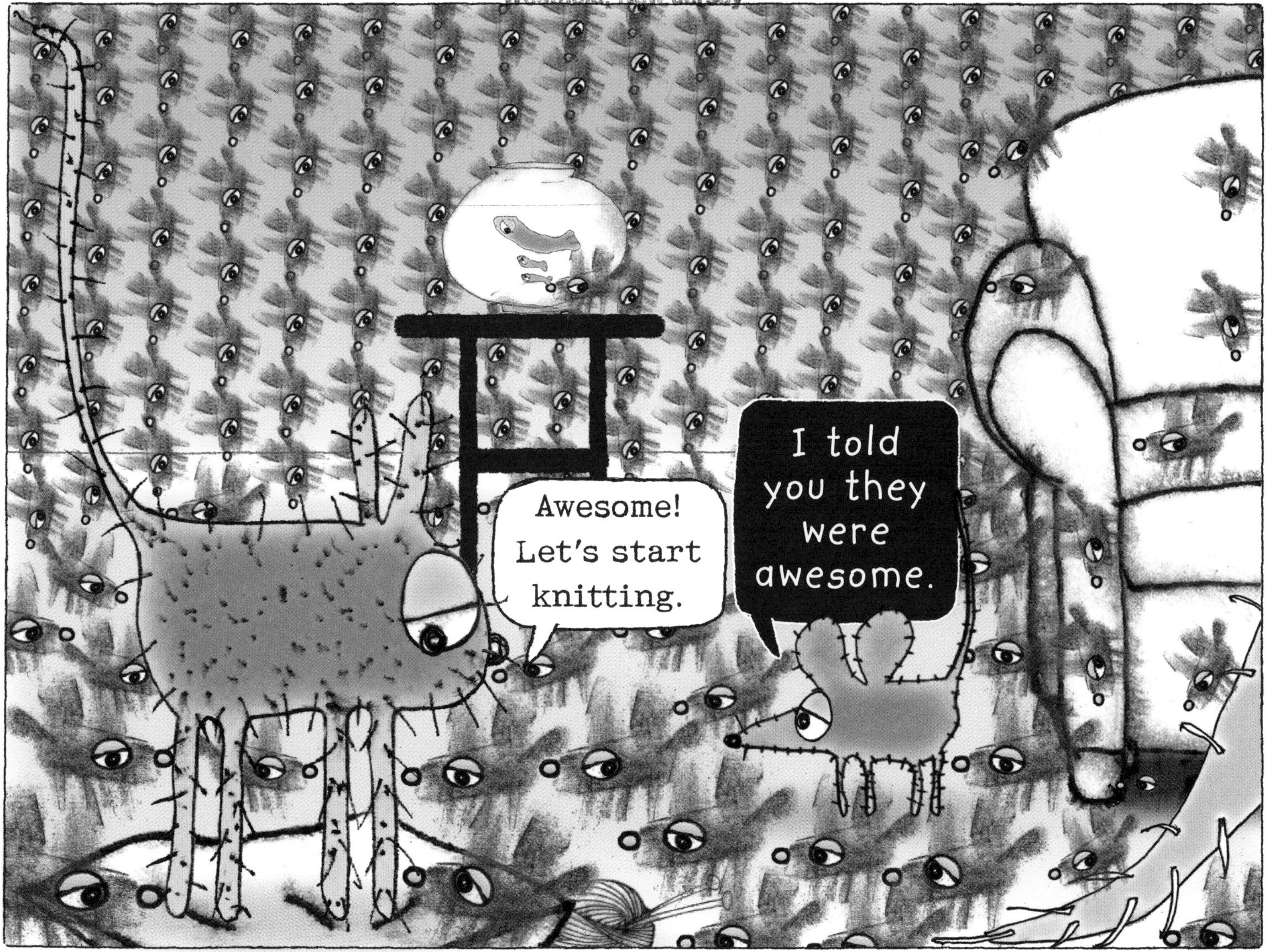
Awesome! Let's start knitting.
I told you they were awesome.